Zip and Zigzag

Written by Catherine Coe
Illustrated by Andy Elkerton

Collins

Pads on, helmets on ...

and go!

Vic zigzags on the bank.

Jess rockets to the hill.

6

Jess is quick.

They jet off.

They zip and kick.

14

15

After reading

Letters and Sounds: Phase 3

Word count: 40

Focus phonemes: /qu/ /j/ /v/ /z/ /th/ /nk/

Common exception words: go, the, to, they, we

Curriculum links: Understanding the World: People and Communities

Early learning goals: Listening and attention: listen to stories, accurately anticipating key events and respond to what is heard with relevant comments, questions or actions; Understanding: answer 'how' and 'why' questions about experiences and in response to stories or events; Reading: read and understand simple sentences; use phonic knowledge to decode regular words and read them aloud accurately; read some common irregular words

Developing fluency

- Your child may enjoy hearing you read the story.
- Model reading a speech bubble (e.g. page 5) with expression. Now read the book with your child, asking them to read all of the speech bubbles with expression.

Phonic practice

Practise reading words that contain new phonemes.

- Say the sounds in the words below.
- Ask your child to repeat the sounds and then say the word.

  qu/i/ck   quick   z/i/p   zip   b/a/nk   bank

- Now read the following two-syllable word, by reading the sounds in each syllable 'chunk' and blending them. Then read each chunk to read the whole word.

  zig/zags

Extending vocabulary

- Ask your child to spot the synonyms below. Which is the odd one out? (*stop*)

  quick   stop   fast

- Look at the 'I spy sounds' pages (14–15). Ask your child how many words they can spot with the /j/ and /v/ sounds in them. (*jelly, juice, jam, jellyfish, jaguar, vest, visor, van, vulture, violin, violets*)